Lesson Learned

∞ #influencer ∞

Lesson Learned

∞ #influencer ∞

Caleb Stark

Published in 2022 by Tswelelo Print
An imprint of Tamarind Hill Press Limited
14023099

ISBN: 978-1-915161-26-0

For bulk orders, contact business@tamarindhillpress.com

TABLE OF CONTENTS

1 6

2 12

3 16

4 20

5 23

ABOUT THE AUTHOR 28

1

"Bro, I can't believe how famous you've become!" Tom said, tapping his co-host on the shoulder and pulling a wide smile from her.

"Me neither, man. It's been crazy," Shane responded, looking between the two hosts.

Shane was participating in his first TV appearance since starting his YouTube channel. He and his best friend, Marcus, created the channel primarily for prank videos, but they occasionally did stunts as well. Shane almost exclusively did all the pranks and stunts while Marcus took care of the video editing and admin work. They gained notoriety after pranking a senator on a live stream, exposing her insatiable and unlawful desire to be with a teenager.

"We have to know," Melinda, Tom's co-host started. "Do you read every comment dropped on your videos? I see some of the ladies posting some pretty scandalous stuff."

Shane laughed. "I read every single one, but it would be a full time job trying to respond to them all, so I rarely say anything back."

"Would you respond if the right woman hit you up? I hear you're single these days."

Melinda lowered her eyes and Shane's mouth went a little dry. He could smell her perfume as it wafted through the air. It made his nose itch a little, but it was a pleasant, floral smell. Even though he could tell her eyelashes were fake, they accentuated the shape of her blue eyes and he liked it. The cherry lip gloss she wore glistened in the bright lights, and it made him wish he could kiss her. For now, though, he settled on answering her question.

"Maybe. I am single, but I'd be more likely to date a TV show host than I would a random YouTube user," Shane said, winking at the end of his sentence.

A few audience members whistled, and Melinda blushed, flipping her brown hair from one side of her head to the other. She smiled deep enough to show her dimples, but before she could respond, Tom cleared his throat.

"Last time I checked, this wasn't a dating show, so let's try to keep things focused on this guy's YouTube channel. Now, there's no need to go into too much detail about all the success the *Sholday* videos have seen, but let's talk a little bit about money," Tom started, giving a playful shrug and grinning to the audience. A few people cheered and clapped as he continued, "I mean, who doesn't like to see them Benjamins?"

The crowd cheered a little more and Shane smiled. He folded his arms and rested his elbows on his knees, looking out at the crowd, soaking in the feeling of being on one of the most popular e-news shows for a moment before responding, "Well, our channel, Sholday, is still pretty new compared to some of the others. I've seen all the likes, and Marcus tells me there's been a ton of money made since our first video went viral late last year."

"So, and excuse me for how blunt I'm being, but exactly how much revenue have you seen since day one?"

The crowd fell silent as they waited for Shane's answer, and it made him a little uncomfortable. He'd never liked talking or even thinking about money, and now he'd been asked to talk about it on a show that would likely be viewed by millions.

"Well, personally, I haven't seen a bunch, but Marcus tells me there will be more coming to me down the line," Shane replied, leaning back and letting the navy sofa cushions relax him a little.

"Seems kind of vague. What kind of deal do you guys have set up?" Melinda chimed in, her cherry lip gloss looking less appetizing by the second.

"I'm not really all that good with numbers, but he tells me we're doing a three quarter split, with it going his way. He said all of the admin and behind the scenes work comes out of my cut though, but since it's a three quarter split, I'll get enough."

Tom chuckled and leaned forward, taking on the posture of a predator stalking its prey.

"Bro, are you sure that's what it is? That sounds like a terrible split. Shouldn't it be a fifty-fifty split since there are two of y'all? With all expenses split too? I mean, really, it should probably be a three quarter split going your way since you do all the stunt, but fifty-fifty still sounds reasonable."

Shane swallowed hard. "Yeah, I'm pretty sure that's what it is. Like I said though, I'm not great with numbers. Isn't three quarters better than fifty-fifty?

The whole crowd laughed, and Shane felt his cheeks flush with embarrassment. His heart started pounding inside his chest and he wanted to disappear into the sofa cushions. Tom and Melinda both slowly shook their heads. The crowd kept laughing for a few more moments before Tom spoke, "Bro, a three quarter split is only good if it's going your way. A fifty-fifty split means it's equal for both of you. Didn't you go to school, man?"

Shane shrugged. "Yeah, but everyone I know said school doesn't really matter until you get to college. I didn't go to college, but I figured it still applied to me."

Melinda kept shaking her head while Tom looked out at the crowd, perking up a little.

"Well, boys and girls, this is a prime example of why you should listen to your parents and not your peers when it comes to school." Tom looked back at Shane with a grin. "Let's forget about all that money talk, since you aren't really making any anyway, and let's talk about the pranks you do. Who comes up with them? Who films?"

Shane answered the questions as best as he could, but he couldn't shake the feeling of embarrassment from the money questions. He spoke to the two hosts on auto pilot, but retreated inside himself to contemplate. He wished he could go back and do the last few years over again. He felt betrayed by Marcus for cheating him out of his money, but more than anything, he felt shame's cold fingers squeezing his chest. He should have known better and now it was too late.

2

On his drive back home, he noticed that the town was bustling with people and overflowing with traffic. Shane just wanted to go home and forget the show ever happened. He came to a red light and his mind began replaying everything that had happened. He still couldn't believe that after all those years together, Marcus would betray him like that.

*Beep! Beep! Beep!

Shane was so lost inside his head he didn't realize that the light had changed. When he looked behind him there was a line forming behind him.

"Alright, alright. I'm going," he uttered furiously, resisting the urge to shout out his window at the honkers.

He drove off and took the right turn home. With the little money that he made from his videos, he was able to afford himself a nice little apartment in a quiet gated community. Shane was quite the celebrity in his neighbourhood. Everyone was always asking for autographs and to take pictures with him.

After buzzing himself in, he made his way down the road, where he passed by a bunch of kids playing on the playground. He reminisced about how carefree he was when he was a child too and was overcome with nostalgia.

Shane grew up in East LA, where poverty and crime were high. He lived with his dad and stepmother, who tried really hard to give him everything so he wouldn't end up on the streets like the other boys in their neighbourhood.

His father worked two jobs so he could afford to send him to an affluent school, where he could learn something and one day be something great and get out of East LA. Shane didn't do too well in school, however. He was more of a class clown. He didn't care much for the classes and would often skip school to hang out with his wealthy friend, Marcus.

Marcus would invite Shane along on his adventures that consisted of getting wasted and partying with rich white kids. He did so many stupid things while hanging out with Marcus and it soon felt like they were just two brothers goofing around.

He thought Marcus was cool because he got to do things that Shane could only dream of. Marcus knew the rich kids in the area and would introduce Shane to them, which eventually led him to meeting the girl that became his first girlfriend.

All of these memories flashed through his mind as he approached his apartment complex. He pulled in his driveway and parked his car next to his neighbour's BMW. He took the key out of the ignition and stepped out of his car. As soon as he opened the front door, he found his neighbour walking into her house.

Her name was Lillian, and she was a house wife. She and her family moved from Boston a few years ago.

Lillian had short jet black hair, dark brown eyes, and a strong jawline. Unlike most women in the neighbourhood, she didn't wear makeup or jewellery and dressed in comfortable clothes that were usually t-shirts and jeans. She was also a big supporter of Shane's YouTube channel.

"Hey Lillian," he said as she entered her house. "You're home early."

She nodded her head and smiled at him. "I'm sorry. Are you okay?"

Shane didn't want to bother his neighbour with his problems, so he just shook his head yes.

Lillian gave him a knowing look and reached out and squeezed Shane's shoulder. "If you change your mind and want to talk about it, I'm here."

Shane gave her a weak smile. "Thanks Lillian."

Lillian turned around and walked into her house. Shane watched her walk away with a heavy heart.

When he got inside, he went straight to his bedroom and flopped on his bed. He was mentally exhausted. He decided he would confront Marcus later after he'd had some rest.

3

In the morning, he woke up to the sound of his phone ringing. He rolled over and checked the screen, seeing that it was Marcus. He picked up the phone without saying anything to see what Marcus wanted.

"Hey, it's Marcus. We need to talk."

Shane sat up and rubbed his face. "Yeah, I guess we do. Where are you?"

Marcus told him that he was out of town on a business trip.

"What kind of business trip? Shouldn't I have known about this trip?" Shane asked his so-called best friend.

Shane became tense as he waited for Marcus to answer.

"It's for some other business I got going on. You don't need to know about everything I do. Anyway, I saw the show."

"Then I think you know you owe me an explanation. How could you do this to me, Marcus? After everything we've been through."

"Listen, Shane. I don't owe you shit, man. If it wasn't for me, this thing wouldn't even have been this big."

"Do you realize how much time and effort I put into that channel? I'm the one who does all the stunts. You took advantage of me. You owe me that money. No way am I going to be cheated out of my fair share."

Marcus scoffed. "I made you. A quarter of what we make is enough for the little part that you play."

"Just tell me how much money I'm owed, and we'll part ways. I can't continue to work with someone who would cheat me like that. Someone I thought I could trust. You were like a brother to me"

Marcus sighed heavily before answering, "It's not much. Just $100,000."

"$100K?! That's it? You expect me to believe that. Do you think I'm stupid, Marcus?" Shane shouted as he got up and paced around.

"Look, I think we both know the answer to that question. I've told you what you're owed and that's that."

"So you're not going to pay me my fair share?"

Marcus laughed. "Fair share? Fair share of what? You think I should pay you half of what I earn? What are you talking about? You don't deserve a penny more. Remember your place, Shane. You're nobody. I just kept you around all these years because I felt sorry for you, Bro. You hear that? You were nothing but a charity case. But I'm done with you."

Shane couldn't believe what Marcus was telling him. His best friend of 10 years used him and was now tossing him away like garbage. It hurt Shane to hear these words coming out of Marcus's mouth. He was a fool for ever thinking that Marcus was his friend. He never cared about him.

He fell back against the wall and placed his head in his hands. "I don't understand, Marcus. Why are you doing this to me?"

"You don't get it, do you? Because a poor rat like you shouldn't be on my level. Never have and you never will. Now, I'm going to go back to my hotel room and enjoy myself while you sit in your apartment crying. Don't worry though, you'll get over it." Marcus let out a sarcastic laugh before the line went dead.

Shane shook his head. Surely, he was in a dream. They must have done something to him at that show. He needed to wake up. There was no way his best friend was doing this to him—treating him like garbage. They had been through too much together. They'd always been there for each other. This had to be a dream, a nightmare even.

He sat staring at the white carpet in his bedroom, trying to make sense of it all. His heart ached.

Shane was now sat in his living room, staring blankly at the television. He had no idea what to do with his life. He felt lost and confused. The only thing that kept him going was his love for making videos and vlogging. He loved filming and editing his videos. He knew it was what he was meant to do. He needed to find another way to make money without involving Marcus.

He didn't know if he could ever forgive Marcus for what he did. Shane felt betrayed and angry at the same time. He couldn't let Marcus get away with what he did to him. He had to make Marcus pay. All those times that Marcus used him for his own gain would come back to haunt him.

He opened the front door and walked outside. He noticed a bunch of children playing on the playground. They were laughing and having fun. He remembered how carefree he was as a kid and longed for those days again.

He walked to the edge of the playground and took a deep breath. Shane felt so alone. He wanted to go back to when he was young and innocent. He wished he could go back in time and redo the past few years.

As Shane looked around, he saw a little girl watching him. She was wearing a green shirt and blue denim shorts. Her hair was blonde and curly, which framed her little face. He noticed that she had a sad expression on her face and tears streaming down her cheeks.

He looked at her and felt compelled to help her. He walked over to the girl and knelt in front of her.

"Are you okay?" he asked her.

She nodded her head yes.

"Why are you crying?" he asked.

The little girl began to cry harder. "My mommy and daddy left me."

Shane felt horrible. He knew exactly how she felt.

"Can I give you a hug?" he asked the girl.

She nodded her head yes.

Shane scooped her up in his arms and held her close to his chest. She buried her face in his neck and cried. Shane hugged her tight and rocked her back and forth.

"It's okay. Everything is going to be alright."

Three days later, Shane heard that Marcus was back in town through a mutual friend. He awoke feeling refreshed and ready to take on the day. He had a lot to do before he confronted Marcus. He decided to start his day with a jog around the park. It would give him the energy he needed to get through the day.

As he jogged, he thought about how he was going to confront Marcus. He decided he would go to his house and confront him there. This way, he would be able to plan his strategy and hopefully put an end to this problem once and for all.

When he got back home, he took a shower and prepared himself for the confrontation. When he finished getting ready, he grabbed his laptop and headed out the door. He drove to Marcus's house and parked in front of the garage. Shane looked around at the community. Every driveway was lined with expensive cars. He simply shook his head.

He walked to the front door and knocked loudly. He heard movement inside and the door opened a crack.

Marcus peeked out at him. "What do you want? What are you even doing here?" he asked rudely.

"We need to talk, Marcus."

Marcus pushed the door open wider and stepped out onto the porch. "Talk about what?"

"About the money you owe me."

Marcus sneered. "I told you, I'm only giving you $100k."

"You don't have to. Keep it. Just sign over the entire business to me and we'll call it even."

"No way!"

"Why not? You've already taken advantage of me. It's time for you to pay up."

"I'm not paying you jack shit!" Marcus shouted.

"Then I guess we'll have to settle this in court," Shane said calmly.

Marcus clenched his fists and shook his head. "Oh, yeah? And why would I settle this in court? You can't prove shit, Shane. You're just a guy from the wrong side of the tracks with an internet personality."

"Because I have proof. I'm sure that the courts would side with me."

Marcus laughed at that. "Well, good luck trying to prove that in court."

"I don't need to prove anything. I simply need to ask to see your bank statements. That should be enough to convince a judge."

"There's nothing to see. You can try to make whatever accusations you want, but it won't work. I'm not signing over any rights to you. I'm not doing anything that would benefit you in any way."

Shane glared at him. "See, Bro, that's where you have things all wrong. I beg to differ."

He reached into his pocket and pulled out his cell phone.

"What are you doing?" Marcus asked.

Shane hit the stop recording button.

"What did you just do?" Marcus asked suspiciously.

"I'm going to post this on YouTube and Facebook. I'm going to tell everyone about what happened between us. I'll also tell them that you lied about everything."

Marcus's face fell, and Shane smiled, "You can't post that, it'll ruin me!" Marcus screamed.

"You haven't been honest with me from the beginning. You've treated me like shit. I don't know what happened between the two of us, but I'm done with you. I'm done trusting people. I'm done working with other people. I don't even want the channel; I'm going to start my own channel and make videos all by myself. This video is just to keep you in check."

"You can't do this to me, Bro. I'm your best friend. We've been best friends for more than 10 years. You're like a brother to me."

It was Shane's turn to laugh. "Brother, right. Brothers don't cheat each other out of their hard earned cash. Brothers don't treat each other like garbage simply because one isn't rich enough. You and I aren't brothers, Marcus. Not anymore. I'll make videos about anything I want. I'll show people what really happens behind closed doors, and how the rich and famous live their lives. I'll expose people for who they truly are, and show them for who they aren't. People like you"

Marcus fell silent.

"Don't ever contact me again, and never get in touch with me in any way, Marcus. I hope you have a nice life."

Marcus turned and walked back into his house. He slammed the door shut and locked it.

Shane never heard from Marcus after that day and he went on to create his own channel, becoming a very successful YouTuber, even more successful than before.

ABOUT THE AUTHOR

Caleb Stark is a fifteen-year-old being raised in a volatile community in Brooklyn, New York. Though he writes fiction, all his stories are influenced by his surroundings. With his short stories, Caleb hopes to teach kids from volatile communities to not allow where they are from or what they have been through to dictate their futures. Caleb wants young people to know that they can break barriers and change their own lives and that of their families.

GET PUBLISHED

Are you a young person, aged between 12 and 17, who writes short stories or other materials such as novels, series, poetry, nonfiction books, etc. and wants to be published?

Contact us at info@tamarindhillpress.co.uk to discuss the possibilities.

TAMARiND HiLL
.PRESS

www.tamarindhillpress.com

YOU MIGHT ALSO LIKE:

www.ingramcontent.com/pod-product-compliance
Lightning Source LLC
Chambersburg PA
CBHW070455170726
48291CB00005B/1763

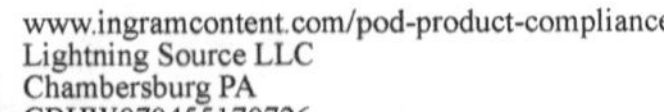